Simpson Snail Sings

by John Himmelman

PUFFIN BOOKS

For Jeff—
keep those great ideas coming!

PUFFIN BOOKS
Published by the Penguin Group
Penguin Books USA Inc., 375 Hudson Street, New York, New York 10014, U.S.A.
Penguin Books Ltd, 27 Wrights Lane, London W8 5TZ, England
Penguin Books Australia Ltd, Ringwood, Victoria, Australia
Penguin Books Canada Ltd, 10 Alcorn Avenue, Toronto, Ontario, Canada M4V 3B2
Penguin Books (N.Z.) Ltd, 182–190 Wairau Road, Auckland 10, New Zealand
Penguin Books Ltd, Registered Offices: Harmondsworth, Middlesex, England

First published in the United States of America by Dutton Children's Books,
a division of Penguin Books USA Inc., 1992
Published in a Puffin Easy-to-Read edition, 1997

1 3 5 7 9 10 8 6 4 2

THE LIBRARY OF CONGRESS HAS CATALOGED THE DUTTON EDITION AS FOLLOWS:
Himmelman, John.
Simpson Snail sings/by John Himmelman.—1st ed.
p. cm.
Summary: Simpson Snail goes to a costume party, makes a new friend, learns to sing, and
sleeps over at Tucker Turtle's house.
ISBN 0-525-44978-7
[1. Snails—Fiction. 2. Animals—Fiction.] I. Title.
PZ7.H5686Si 1992 91–46955 CIP AC
[E]—dc20

Puffin Easy-to-Read ISBN 0-14-038434-0

Puffin® and Easy-to-Read® are registered trademarks of Penguin Books USA Inc.

Printed in the United States of America

Reading Level 1.6

Contents

Super Snail

Simpson Snail

was going

to a costume party.

He got out his costume.

He was very happy.

"I am going to be Super Snail,"

he said.

"No one will know

I am Simpson."

He went to the party.

Everyone had nice costumes.

"Hello, Simpson,"

said a ghost.

"I am not Simpson.

I am Super Snail,"

said the snail.

A witch walked up.

"How are you, Simpson?"

she asked.

"There is no Simpson here,"

said the snail.

"Good to see you, Simpson,"

said a spaceman.

"Simpson? Is Simpson here?"

asked the snail.

This is not fun,

thought Simpson.

Everyone knows who I am.

Then someone dressed as a flower

walked up to him.

"What a nice costume.

Who are you?"

asked the flower.

"Oh, you know it is me.

I am Simpson Snail."

"Don't you know who I am?"

asked the flower.

She took off her hat and mask.

It was Gypsy Moth.

Gypsy was Simpson's good friend.

"Come with me," she said.

"I will help you

with your costume.

Then no one will know

you are Simpson Snail."

They went into another room.

Simpson crawled out of his shell.

Gypsy worked on his costume.

Soon they came out again.

"Hello, Simpson,"

said a monster.

Super Snail said nothing.

"Good to see you, Simpson,"

said a pirate.

Super Snail said nothing.

"Your shell gives you away, Simpson,"

said a clown.

Super Snail said nothing.

Soon it was time

for the prizes.

Everyone gathered around.

"The first prize

for the best disguise

goes to the flower,"

said the host.

Off came the flower's mask.

It was Simpson!

"If you are Simpson,

then who is that?"

The host pointed to Super Snail.

Out of the Super Snail costume came...

Gypsy!

Everyone cheered.

"The first prize

will go to both

Simpson *and* Gypsy,"

said the host.

And Simpson and Gypsy

were happy to share it.

Simpson's Fortune

Gypsy loved to tell fortunes.

She told Simpson his fortune.

"You will make a new friend,"

she said.

"But you will lose a friend, too."

"Oh, no!" said Simpson.

"I do not want to lose a friend!"

Simpson was not happy.

He went for a walk.

"Hello," said Lady Bug.

"You look sad.

Do you want to hear a joke?"

"Okay," said Simpson.

"Why did the spider

cross the road?"

asked Lady.

"I don't know," said Simpson.

"To get to the other side!"

said Lady.

Simpson laughed.

"That is funny," he said.

"Feel better?" asked Lady.

"A little," said the snail.

"Good," said Lady Bug.

"And thanks for laughing.

I like to tell jokes,

but no one ever laughs at them."

"I will laugh at your jokes,"

said Simpson.

Then Simpson saw

Woolly Caterpillar.

Maybe Woolly is the friend

Gypsy said I would lose,

he thought.

He left Lady Bug.

"Are we still friends?"

Simpson asked Woolly.

"Of course!" said Woolly.

"Good," said Simpson.

Simpson went back

to Lady Bug.

"Please tell me

another joke," he said.

"Okay," said Lady Bug.

"Why did the bee

throw his clock out the window?"

"Why?" asked Simpson.

"He wanted to see time fly!"

said Lady.

Simpson laughed again.

"You are very funny,"

he said.

But then Simpson saw

Carpenter Ant.

Maybe Carpenter is the friend

I will lose,

he thought.

He went off to see the ant.

"Are we still friends?"

Simpson asked.

"Sure," said Carpenter.

"Good," said Simpson.

"I should go back

to Lady Bug.

She will think

that I do not like her."

But Simpson was too late.

Lady Bug was gone.

"Oh, no!" said Simpson.

"I have lost her!"

Simpson went to see Gypsy.

Gypsy was not alone.

She was with Lady Bug!

"Oh, Gypsy,"

said Simpson.

"You were right.

I made a friend and I lost a friend.

And they were both Lady Bug!"

"That is all right," said Lady.

"Gypsy told my fortune, too,"

Lady went on.

"She said that I will

find a lost friend."

"Am I a lost friend?"

asked Simpson.

"No," said Lady.

"Now you are a found friend!"

Snail Song

Simpson loved mornings.

Everyone sang

in the morning.

Everyone except Simpson.

Simpson did not know

how to sing.

"I will learn

how to sing,"

he said.

"I will find

the best singers.

Maybe they can teach me."

He found Redwing Blackbird.

"KEEE-ooo-REEEEE,"

sang the bird.

"Can you teach me

to sing like that?"

asked Simpson.

"Just open your beak,"

said Redwing.

"And sing from your belly."

Simpson tried it.

"KEEEOOP!"

he shouted.

"I guess you have to

be a bird to sing,"

said Redwing.

"I will try something easier,"

said Simpson.

He found Spring Peeper.

"PEEP, PEEP, PEEP,"

sang Spring Peeper.

His throat puffed way out.

"So that is the secret,"

said Simpson.

He tried it.

"Gug, gug, gug,"

croaked Simpson.

"This will not do,"

said the snail.

"You need to be a peeper,"

said Spring Peeper.

Simpson went to see

Grace Hopper.

"You make nice music,"

said the snail.

"Can you teach me?"

"It is easy,"

said the grasshopper.

"Just rub your legs

on your wings.

Skrip, skrip, skrip,"

went the grasshopper.

"I do not have wings,"

said Simpson.

"But I will use my shell."

Simpson tried.

It did not work.

He made no noise at all.

"You have to be a grasshopper,"

said Grace.

Simpson was sad.

Then he saw Lady Bug.

"I wish I could sing

like everyone else,"

he told her.

"But you are not everyone else,"

she said.

"You are Simpson Snail.

Sing a Simpson Snail song."

"I will try," said Simpson.

"I AM SIMPSON.

I AM A SNAIL.

I LIKE TO LAUGH

AT LADY'S JOKES.

I LIKE TO SING."

Redwing Blackbird,

Spring Peeper,

and Grace Hopper

heard Simpson.

"That was nice!"

they said.

"Can you teach us

to sing like that?"

"I don't think so,"

said Simpson proudly.

"You need to be a snail."

Simpson's Sleepover

Simpson packed his bag.

He was going to

Tucker Turtle's house.

I have never slept over

at a friend's house before,

thought Simpson.

He was very excited.

At Tucker's house

they ate dinner.

Then they played some games.

"We should sleep now,"

said Tucker.

"We can play more

in the morning."

Tucker got in his bed.

Simpson got in his bed.

Tucker fell asleep.

Simpson was wide awake.

He wanted to play more games.

"Tucker, wake up,"

said Simpson.

"Snore, snore,"

said Tucker.

Simpson stayed awake all night.

In the morning,

he was too tired to play.

"You can sleep over again tonight,"

said Tucker.

Simpson went home.

I will stay up all day,

he thought.

Then I will be tired

at night.

I won't stay awake

all night, tonight.

Tucker was thinking, too.

I will sleep all day,

he thought.

Then I can stay awake

with Simpson tonight.

That night,

Simpson went to Tucker's.

They played some fun games.

Then Tucker got in his bed.

And Simpson got in his bed.

Now Tucker was wide awake.

But Simpson fell fast asleep.

"Wake up and play," said Tucker.

"Snore, snore," said Simpson.

In the morning,

Tucker was too tired to play.

"This is not working,"

said Simpson.

"Tonight, we will *both*

stay awake."

That night

Simpson sat in his bed.

Tucker sat in his bed.

"If I fall asleep,

you make a noise.

If you fall asleep,

I will make a noise.

The noises

will keep us awake,"

said Simpson.

Tucker started to fall asleep.

Simpson made a noise.

Tucker woke up.

Simpson started to fall asleep.

Tucker made a noise.

Simpson woke up.

They stayed awake all night long.

"This is fun," said Tucker.

"But I am getting tired."

"Me, too," said Simpson.

"Let's both go to sleep.

We can play in the morning."

Simpson fell asleep.

Tucker fell asleep.

And in the morning,

it was time to play.

But Simpson and Tucker

slept some more.